MP…TAP!

THUD-THUMP…TAP!

THUD-THUMP…TAP!

THUD-THUMP...TAP! THUD-THUMP...TAP!

Dedicated to Danab, Kodi, Kian, Willan & Kyle

Tricycle Press
P.O. Box 7123
Berkeley, California 94707
www.tenspeed.com

Book design by Susan Van Horn
Typeset in Deepdene and Windsor Antique

Library of Congress Cataloging-in-Publication Data
McFarland, Lyn Rossiter.
The pirate's parrot / Lyn Rossiter McFarland; illustrations, Jim McFarland.
p.   cm.
Summary: Filling in for Captain Cur's dead parrot, Barr the teddy
bear proves herself to be a brave and useful companion to the pirate.
ISBN 1-58246-014-0 (hardcover)
[1. Pirates Fiction.   2. Teddy bears Fiction.]
I. McFarland, Jim, ill.   II. Title.
PZ7.R72247Pi   2000
[Fic]—dc21   99-38357
CIP

First printing, 2000.
Printed in Hong Kong

1 2 3 4 5 6 7 — 04 03 02 01 00

THE
PIRATE'S PARROT

October 6, 2001

Enjoy me book!

Jim McFarland

WRITTEN BY

LYN ROSSITER MCFARLAND

ILLUSTRATIONS BY

JIM MCFARLAND

TRICYCLE PRESS

Berkeley, California

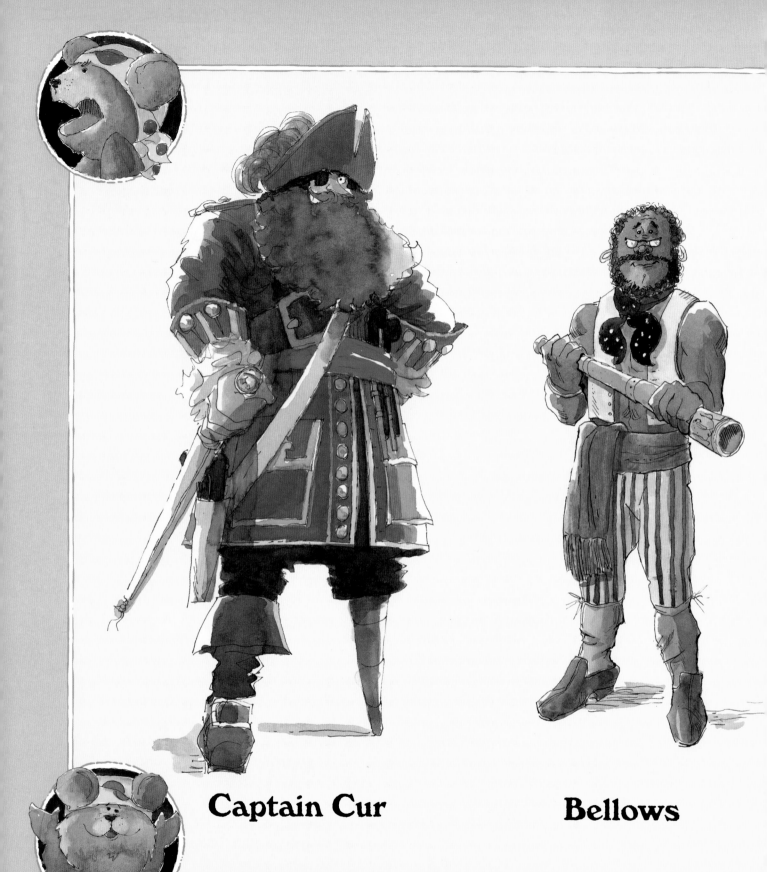

Captain Cur

Bellows

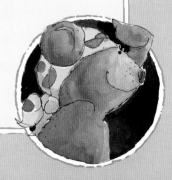

Spittleton   Loot

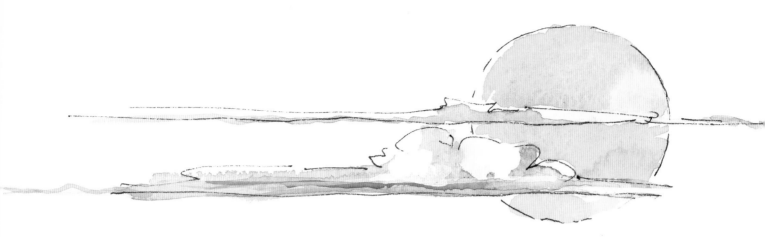

THUD-THUMP...TAP!

TAP! TAP!

THUD-THUMP...TAP!

When Captain Cur's parrot died, he thud-thumped and tapped on his wooden leg all night long, until his crew thought they'd go mad.

Then, at dawn, he tap, tap, crunched! "Mr. Bellows!" he roared. "I've stepped on me monocle!"

Quartermaster Bellows rushed to his captain's side.

"I have no bird," snarled the Cur. "I have no monocle. Me near vision's a blur, and me mood is bad and getting worse. So what are you going to do about it?"

CRUNCH!

That night Bellows
sent First Mate Spittleton
and Second Mate Loot
ashore to shoplift a bird
and a monocle.
They returned to
the *Mongrel* at sunup
with a box of booty.
"'Tis me new bird?" asked the Cur, as
he ripped open the box, yanked out what
was inside, and plunked it down upon
his shoulder.

The pirates gasped. It wasn't a bird. It was a teddy bear!

"And now me new monocle!" demanded the Cur.

"They had none," lied Loot, as he slipped the stolen eyepiece into his pocket.

"Blast!" thundered Captain Cur. "Well then, how does me new bird look, mates?"

He leaned forward.

The teddy slipped off his shoulder, bounced down the stairs, and landed at the pirates' feet.

The pirates snickered. They chuckled. They clutched their sides and howled with laughter.

"What be that sound?" asked Captain Cur.

"'Tis the dreaded 'giggles of fear,'" said Bellows. "Why your bird leapt at the men, and they be afeared of it."

"It be a strange bird," said the Cur, "that strikes such fear."

Bellows picked the teddy up. "Aye, it's a real fur-feathered, sharp-toothed, beady-eyed buzzard of a bird," he said.

"Well, whatever it is," said the Cur, "teach it its duties."

"Aye, sir," said Bellows, as the Cur went below.

"Guess we stole the wrong box," said Loot.

"Aye," said Spittleton.

"Toss it overboard," said Bellows.

Loot grabbed the teddy.

The teddy grabbed Loot!

"It's got me!" Loot shrieked, shaking his arm. "Let go!"

"No," squeaked the teddy, "I can't swim!"

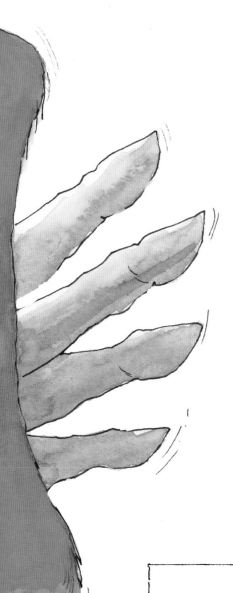

"You can speak?" said Bellows. He pried the bear off Loot's fingers.

"Aye," said the teddy. "I'm a walking, talking teddy bear."

"Aye, 'tis a wonder," Bellows said. "Yet our Captain needs a seeing-eye polly for his blind side, especially since he has no monocle. So you be a pirate's parrot for now, name of Barr."

"Barr it is," said Barr.

"Good boy," said Bellows.

"Good *girl*," said Barr.

"A girlie teddy!" sputtered Loot. "Aboard a pirate ship! What if she can't squawk the warning for our Captain?"

"Squawk," ordered Bellows.

Barr squawked.

"Excellent squawking," said Spittleton.

"Ha!" snorted Loot. "There's more to being a pirate's parrot than a squawk. Pirates swagger, swashbuckle, and bite. And give the evil eye."

SQUAWK!

"And spit," said Spittleton. And Spittleton spat a sticky glob of spit, right onto Loot's shiny head.

Bellows dressed Barr in pirate gear and handed her a small hook.

"Now practice," he said.

So Barr bit and spit. And screeched and squawked. And swaggered and swashbuckled. And hooked her way up Loot's pants and perched on his shoulder.

"Excellent perching," said Spittleton.

"Good enough," said Bellows.

"Mates," said Bellows, "meet the Captain's new parrot."

"But, it's the teddy!" cried the pirates.

"And who wants to tell the Cur his parrot be a teddy?" asked Bellows.

Just then the ship's lookout shouted, "Ship ahoy! Merchant ship to starboard!"

"Mr. Bellows!" roared the Cur as he thud-thump tapped up the stairs. "I need me bird!"

Barr's paws shook, but Spittleton gave her a pat.

Bellows gave her a smile. "Don't worry, you can do it," he whispered. "It's only for a short while, 'til we find a real bird."

Bellows set Barr up on her Captain's shoulder.

Barr hung on tight as the pirates caught the merchant ship with grappling hooks and pulled alongside.

"Find me a monocle," ordered Captain Cur.

"And a bird," muttered Bellows.

"Aye, aye," cried the pirates.

"No prey, no pay!" the Cur shouted, and the pirates jumped onto the merchant ship.

"Ye sniveling lickspittles!" snarled the Cur at the merchant ship's sailors.

"You silly spitlicks!" sqawked Barr. She twirled her hook and spat. A sticky glob of spit hit the Cur's beard.

He didn't notice, but the merchant sailors did. They snickered. They chuckled. They clutched their sides and howled with laughter. They gasped for breath. All surrendered.

"Could this be the dreaded 'giggles of fear'?" asked the Cur.

"Aye, sir," said Bellows.

And so it went with every ship the pirates boarded. They seized a great deal of treasure, but found no bird. And no new monocle.

"This playing a pirate is fun," said Barr.

"You're no pirate," grumbled Loot. "Real pirates fight and save their mates and seize treasure. All you do is sit on a shoulder."

"Aye," said Bellows. "Someday the Captain will see you for what you are."

Barr hung her head and said nothing.

Then one day the lookout shouted, "Ship ahoy, dead ahead!" It was a warship—the *Sea Weasel.*

Barr had never seen anything so big.

"No prey, no pay!" shouted the Cur as he jumped onto the *Sea Weasel's* deck, right into...

CAPTAIN McDAGGER!

Barr gasped.

McDagger had a *parrot!*

Captain McDagger leapt

forward and slashed at the Cur.

The Cur snapped back!

Barr lost her balance and slammed into the Cur's face.

"Blasted bird!" cried Captain Cur. Before he could peel her off, McDagger clobbered him from behind.

Barr fell as the Cur hit the deck.

"You're my prisoner now," sneered McDagger.

"Leave me Captain alone," yelled Barr. She hooked her way up McDagger's coat and onto his shoulder. She spat a sticky glob of spit into his eyes. Then she hooked her hook through McDagger's earring and yanked, hard.

"Owww!" McDagger howled, as the earring tore free. He swung at Barr with his sword and sliced off the tip of her ear!

"Leave me bird alone!" roared Captain Cur, as he heaved himself up off the deck. He grabbed McDagger and kicked him overboard.

"Back to the *Mongrel!*" he ordered, just as Loot caught McDagger's parrot.

"Leave that!" bellowed the Cur.

Loot did.

Soon the pirates
were safely away.
"Will you look at this,"
said the Cur. He held up
McDagger's earring.
"Never had a bird
do such a fighting thing
before." He poked the
earring into Barr's ear.

Barr touched it with her paw.

"'Tis beautiful," said Spittleton.

"'Tis pure gold," sighed Loot, a tear coming to his eye. He pulled his pirate's kerchief from his pocket and as he did, something fell out and bounced on the deck.

"What be this?" said Captain Cur, bending to pick it up. "A monocle?"

Loot gulped.

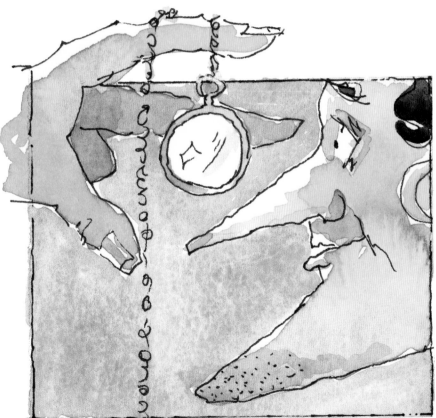

Captain Cur put it on. He looked at Barr. He looked at his crew.
He smiled a smile that shivered their spines and tingled their toes.

"So, how does me bird look now, mates?" he asked.

The pirates froze.

"And just what manner of bird did you say it be, Mr. Bellows?"

But before Bellows could answer, Barr crowed, **"I am a fur-feathered, sharp-toothed, beady-eyed buzzard of a bird, me Captain, sir!"**

"That ye be," said Captain Cur. He scratched Barr's head. "Now, look alive. We've ships to sink and gold to grab!"

"No prey, no pay!" cried Barr.

"Aye, mates," said Captain Cur. "You heard me bird. No prey, no pay!"

"Aye!" cried the pirates.

"Aye!" cried Bellows, Spittleton, and Loot, as the *Mongrel* headed out into the open sea.